D1314955

The Boo Crew

adapted by Kara McMahon
based on the screenplay "The Funnyman Boogeyman"
written by Rodney Stringfellow
illustrated by Carlo Lo Raso

Ready-to-Read

SIMON SPOTLIGHT / NICK JR.
New York   London   Toronto   Sydney

Based on the TV series *Nick Jr. The Backyardigans*™ as seen on Nick Jr.™

SIMON SPOTLIGHT
An imprint of Simon & Schuster Children's Publishing Division
1230 Avenue of the Americas, New York, New York 10020
© 2010 Viacom International Inc. All rights reserved. NICKELODEON, NICK JR., *Nick Jr. The Backyardigans*,
and all related titles, logos, and characters are trademarks of Viacom International Inc.
The Backyardigans is co-produced in association with Nelvana. NELVANA™ Nelvana Limited. CORUS™ Corus
Entertainment Inc. All rights reserved, including the right of reproduction in whole or in part in any form.
SIMON SPOTLIGHT, READY-TO-READ, and colophon are registered trademarks of Simon & Schuster, Inc.
For information about special discounts for bulk purchases, please contact Simon & Schuster Special Sales at
1-866-506-1949 or business@simonandschuster.com.
Manufactured in the United States of America 0610 LAK
First Edition
2 4 6 8 10 9 7 5 3 1
Library of Congress Cataloging-in-Publication Data
McMahon, Kara.
The Boo Crew / adapted by Kara McMahon. — 1st ed.
p. cm. — (Ready-to-read)
"Based on the screenplay 'The Funnyman Boogeyman' written by Rodney Stringfellow."
"Based on the TV series ... The Backyardigans as seen on Nick Jr."—T.p. verso.
ISBN 978-1-4169-9751-1
I. Backyardigans (Television program) II. Title. PZ7.M478752Bo 2010
[E]—dc22
2009042725

I am !
UNIQUA

And I am !
PABLO

We are the Boo Crew!

It is our job to catch

spooky creatures.

"We are not afraid
of anything," says .

UNIQUA

"We are not afraid

of , or  , or  ,"

GHOSTS   VAMPIRES   GOBLINS

says  .

PABLO

Nothing scares the Boo Crew!

We are brave!

We have cool GADGETS.

We have training.

We say, "Boo!"

We are the Boo Crew!

Today we want to catch the spookiest creature of all!

Is it a  ? NO!
GHOST

Is it a ? NO!
VAMPIRE

Is it a ? NO!
GOBLIN

It is the  **BOOGEYMAN**!

Do not be scared!

You are safe with us!

We are the Boo Crew!

Where is the  BOOGEYMAN hiding?
We think he is at
the haunted THEATER .
We will drive the Boo Crew
 VAN to the haunted THEATER .

It is spooky inside the !
THEATER

Look at the !
COBWEBS

Our cool will help us
GADGETS

find the .
BOOGEYMAN

Our  have sensors.
GADGETS
BEEP!
Our sense that
GADGETS
the is near.
BOOGEYMAN

"I see a ," says  .
DOOR PABLO

"Over there!

Maybe that is where

the  is hiding!"
BOOGEYMAN

says  .
UNIQUA

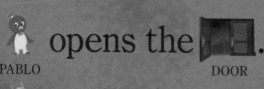 opens the .

PABLO DOOR

 walks in.

UNIQUA

"Boo!" yells .

UNIQUA

 is right behind her.

PABLO

Is the  inside?

BOOGEYMAN

There is no inside!
BOOGEYMAN

There is no inside.
VAMPIRE

There is no inside.
GHOST

There is no inside.
GOBLIN

Nothing spooky is inside!

"Did you hear that?"

asks .

UNIQUA

"Did I hear what?" asks .

PABLO

Then they both hear it!

"Find me!" calls a voice.

"Find me now," yells the voice.

"I think that is the 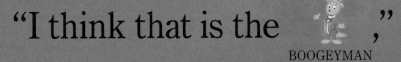 ,"
BOOGEYMAN

says  .
UNIQUA

"He WANTS us to find him?"

asks  .
PABLO

"That is strange!"

"Boo!" yells .
UNIQUA

"Boo!" yells 🐧.
PABLO

"We are coming

to catch you!"

The  drops in

BOOGEYMAN

from the ceiling!

"Did I make you laugh?"

asks the .

BOOGEYMAN

 and are not laughing.

UNIQUA   PABLO

"Take cover!" yells .
PABLO

They hide behind a .
CHAIR

"How will we catch him?"

whispers .
UNIQUA

What will the Boo Crew do?

"Can we play again?"

asks the  .
BOOGEYMAN

"The  thinks
BOOGEYMAN

we are playing!" says .
PABLO

The  is not scary at all!
BOOGEYMAN

"We are sorry we wanted to catch you," says  .
UNIQUA

"We are the Boo Crew!"

The BOOGEYMAN understands.

He just wants to play!

GROWL!

"What was that?" yells  PABLO.

"That was just my tummy,"
says the  .
BOOGEYMAN

It is time for a snack!